DATE DUE		

A Dime a Dozen

NIKKI GRIMES

A Dime a Dozen

Pictures by ANGELO

DIAL BOOKS FOR YOUNG READERS

New York

Published by Dial Books for Young Readers
A member of Penguin Group (USA) Inc.
345 Hudson Street
New York, New York 10014

Text copyright © 1998 by Nikki Grimes
Pictures copyright © 1998 by Angelo
All rights reserved
Designed by Nancy R. Leo
Printed in Mexico on acid-free paper
First Edition
3 5 7 9 10 8 6 4

Library of Congress Cataloging in Publication Data
Grimes, Nikki.
A dime a dozen/ Nikki Grimes; pictures by Angelo.
p. cm.
Summary: A collection of poems about
an African-American girl growing up in New York City.
ISBN 0-8037-2227-3 (trade)
1. Afro-Americans—Juvenile poetry. 2. Children's poetry, American.
[1. Afro-Americans—Poetry. 2. American poetry.]
I. Angelo, date, ill. II. Title.
PS3557.R489982D56 1998   811'.54—dc21   97-5798   CIP   AC

The translation for the Spanish words in *Yo te amo* is
"I love you with/all my heart."

For my father, James,
who told me that I was one of a kind

—N.G.

To my three musketeers—
Vickie, Pam, and Gwen

—A.

Contents

Where Do Writers Come From?

I get all sorts of questions when I visit schools or speak at young writers conferences these days. Most people want to know what my background is, who inspired or influenced me, and how I came to be a writer.

So lately I've been thinking a lot about my childhood, my family, and the events—both good and bad—which have helped shape me. I've chosen a few of them to write about in this collection. These poems answer some of the most commonly asked questions, like: Did I become a writer because everyone thought I'd be good at it?

By the way, the answer to that one is NO! My mother thought it was a horrible idea, and the people in my neighborhood said, "Writers don't come from 'round here!"

Looks like they were wrong, doesn't it? That just goes to show, it pays to listen to your own heart!

PART I : *Genius*

The Dream

Oh! To poet
like a laser,
pierce darkness
with one word!

Stroll

Every time
we go walking
my long legs
gobble up
the distance
four times as fast
as Mom's
short stems.

"Wait up," she begs,
 suggesting that
we match
our steps.

            But

I set my own pace
'cause Spirit says
I'm heading places
that aren't marked
on my mother's

            map.

On Quiet Feet

When my dad walks
into a room,
or down
the street,
he inches
up on me
silent
as shadow,
and I don't know
he's there
until I feel
his hug.

Sometimes
when he is
near
I might even
hear
his heart beat—
but never
his quiet
feet.

Hopscotch

His too-big feet
fill the chalk square
of my hopscotch box
but he doesn't care
or seem to notice
the kids across the street
laughing out loud
each time his size tens
spill over the white line.
"You doin' just fine,"
I tell him, and wink.
I'll keep my dad, I think.

Handel

Some evenings
my father prays before
his music stand
and lays hands
on his violin
as if the wood
were holy.

We, silent
by the stereo,
relax while
Handel preaches
a sermon-song
through piccolo,
cello and bass,
trombone and kettledrum.

I fold my hands
and hum
until the music fades.
Then Daddy gently
lifts his bow
and plays
a violin solo.

He shatters
heaven's crystal floor
with melody
that rings so pure
the angels pause
to listen while
I whisper,
That's my daddy!

Music Lesson

The choir paints
    the sanctuary walls
with bands of sound
    more glorious than gold

And all around
    the altar, voices raise
in matchless harmonies
    of perfect praise—

Perfect, except
    for Mom, who tonelessly
expands the meaning of
    the phrase "off-key."

She swears I'll miss
    her singing when she's gone.
Says she, "Not all folks get
    the gift of song."

That may be true,
    But miss her singing? *Wrong.*

Hair Prayer

I used to brush
her long black waves
each day until they'd shine,

        And ask the Lord
        for hair like Mom's
        instead of hair like mine.

"I wish I had
your short tight curls,"
Mom said to me one day.

        "They frame your face
        so perfectly.
          I can't get mine that way."

I guess I'll keep
the hair I have.
To change it would be wrong.
It suits me rather well. Of course,
        I knew that all along.

Yo te amo

Maybe there's some
scientific reason
she gets the urge to hug
whenever we're
jammed together
in the rush-hour huddle.

Thank God, she knows better
than to cuddle—in public.
Instead, while the train
screeches to the next station
she leans down
to whisper in my ear
Yo te amo con
todo mi corazón.
If no one else can hear
I figure it's okay
      to smile.

Don't ask me
who she learned
that expression from
but someone
must've told my mom
that Spanish is
the language of love
        'cause
she's been speaking
mushy Puerto Rican
        to me
        for years.

Gin Rummy

If I could choose
I'd never lose
a game of cards.
But every time
Mom wants to play
I play.

More times than not
my mother's luck
is running hot,
while mine is
icy cold.

When I am old
perhaps I will
admire Mother's
proven skill.
But now. . .

I must confess
I'm honestly
my happiest
when Mother
lets me win
a hand or two
of gin.

Second Mother

Stop calling me your "baby."
Don't call me "Little Bit."
Every time I
hear those words
I grind my teeth
and spit.

> Besides,
> I've got
> a proper name—
> and Baby
> isn't it!

Stop calling me your "baby."
Don't call me "Little Miss."
You're not my
mother anyway.
Remember? You're
my *sis!*

Sister's Skin

Her velvet skin's
       an
       ebon
       hue

In summer sun
       it's
       nearly
       blue

I once dreamt I
       was
       dark
       as
       she

And
       E v e r y b o d y
       envied
       Me.

Genius

"Sis! Wake up!" I whisper
in the middle of the night.

> Urgently I shake her
> till she switches on the light.

The spiral notebook in my hand
provides her quick relief.

> It tells her there's no danger
> of a break-in by a thief.

"Okay," she says, then props herself
up vertically in bed.

> She nods for me to read my work.
> I cough, then forge ahead.

The last verse of my poem leaves
her silent as a mouse.

> I worry till she says, "We have
> a genius in the house."

PART II : *The Secret*

Daddy's Promises

"We'll go to the zoo,"
  you said
"I'll come by at two,"
  you said
  I sat by the door
  to wait
  The evening hour
  grew late
  I cried in bed
  again
  and wondered if
  or when
  you'd learn to keep
  your promises

Less Than Perfect

A half-empty bottle
of blackberry brandy
drips its
sticky poison
on Mother's nightstand.
She waves me
to my room
with trembling hand
and, like always, says
"Mommy's just
tired, honey."
So I pretend not to see
the berry-stained
shot glass
within her anxious
grasp.

Travelin' Man

We're on the road
just Dad and me
in his dusty black MG.
We're going
it doesn't matter where
as long as we go there
together.
Sometimes
when he leaves alone
I worry that
he might be gone
forever.

Mother's Best Friend

When Ruby comes
she flips my mother's
giggle switch,
       and soon
Mom's shadow of a grin
brightens into
a smile so wide
I could dive
into her dimples
and disappear
       for days
and not be missed.

How could this
be the person
who hides inside
my mother's skin?

Maybe next time
Ruby comes
she'll leave this
laughing mom
       behind
a little longer
       for me.

Empty Pockets

I used to wish
Dad would stop
gambling
with his
borrowed
money
and Mom's
buried
love.

Foster Home

I remember one foster home
how the mom reached out
      that first day
and gathered me in her arms

      how I pulled away
unable to explain that her
comforting embrace felt like
      borrowed love

and I was afraid to slip it on
like a warm coat in winter
      just in case
      she might later
tap me on the shoulder
      demanding
      its return.

Untitled

It happened
  to Maria
Malik
  and Danny Gold;

To Javier
  and Suki
Jim Roth
  and Suzy Chow.

My parents
  got divorced
  last month

    . . . I guess
    I fit in now.

The Secret

She thinks I don't see her
staring after Dad
when he walks out
the door but
I do. I catch him too
sneaking a lonely
peek at Mom
out the corner of his eye.
Why can't they see
how much they still
want to be
together?

Morning Menu

"Dad, you are hopeless
   in the kitchen,"
I tease every time
I come to visit.
Then I make him sit
at the table
while I sizzle up bacon
and fry eggs over easy
like Mom taught me.
And it's a good thing
'cause Dad is nothing
but bones and skin—
especially thin
for someone
six feet tall,
and all he knows
about cooking
is that the word
begins with C.
That's why
he needs
Me.

PART III : *A Dime a Dozen*

The Last Word

I peeled several potatoes
and tossed them in a pot.

Chop!

Said Grandma, "You should boil them first,
then peel them while they're hot."

Chop! Chop!

When they were done, I cubed them
into pieces one-inch thick.

Chop!

"No! No!" said she. "You slice them fine.
Like *so.* I know the trick."

Chop! Chop!

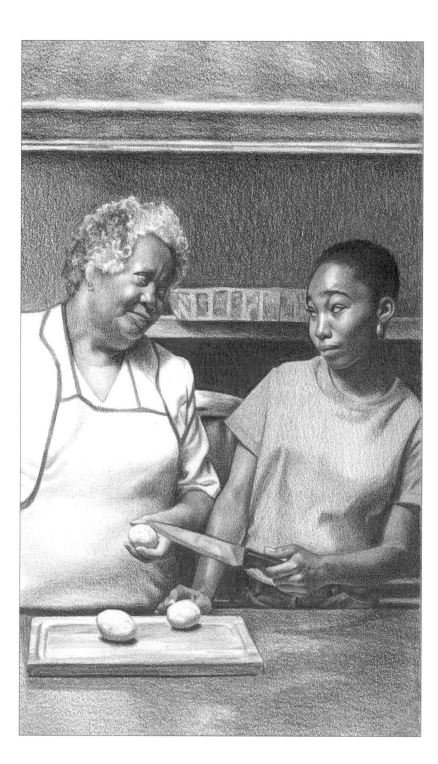

"This *recipe* is *mine*," I said.
  (As if she cared a lick!)

Chop!

"Just do it my way. Do it right.
  Here! Hand me the knife!

Chop! Chop!

"You'd better learn to cook well
  if you want to be a wife."

Chop! Chop!

"I'll have you know, I've made
  this salad many times before.

Chop!

"I'm grateful for your help
  but I don't need it anymore."

Chop!

"No need to get all huffy,"
  said she, handing back the knife.

Chop! Chop!

I asked, "Oh, by the way,
  who said I planned to be a wife?"

Chop!

Soul Food

"Soul food is really
  not my thing.
  I have no taste
  for chitterlings,

  though black-eyed peas
  and rice are nice,"
  I told my mom
  when I was young.

"I don't eat ox-
  tail soup or tongue,
  but yams, collard
  greens, and kale—

Mmm, mmm, mmm!

                         Lordy-Lord!

  Just don't cook them
  in fatback
  because I don't
  eat Black."

Bilingual

My girlfriend
Guadalupe knows
she's not
the only one
who speaks
two tongues.
I'm fluent in
two Englishes:
      one "Black"
      the other "good."
It pays to speak
both languages
in my neighborhood.

Self

When I grow up
I want to be
like my old man
who is his own
from his out-of-style
black beret
to his soft-as-butter
leather loafers.

Something New

Grandma used to sit
in her vinylized chair
wire-rim glasses on
the tip of her nose
teasing gravity

and she'd surrender
to Spillane or
Agatha Christie
for the night.
On the doilied

table beside her
haloed in lamplight
would be her Bible
alongside Webster's tome
kept handy just in case

her murder mystery
should yield some
new word-treasure.
She'd be equipped
to find and measure

its meaning before
adding it to her massive
collection. Still, "You're
never too old to learn
something new," wasn't

tattooed on my memory
until the day
my grandmother
turned sixty
and earned her G. E. D.

Family Movers

REMEMBER
>   First, bend at the knee.

BACK STRAIGHT.
>   Wait till the count of three.

THEN LIFT!
>   Don't scuff the parquet floor.

CAREFUL!
>   Ease it through the door.

HEADS UP!
>   Time to turn around.

THERE!
>   Now, lower and set it down.

SIS SAYS
>   When there's work to be done

BECOME
>   A handywoman.

A Dime a Dozen

Writers are   a dime a dozen
                      a dime a dozen
                      a dime—

I heard those words one time too many

from my own mother who
worried I would fail and said
"Find another dream instead."

But my heart scripted one phrase truer:

"Someday she'll   be proud to say
                     be proud to say
                     be proud—

To shout out loud   *My daughter,*
                     the Writer."

A Note About the Author

Nikki Grimes started out on her path as a writer by ignoring most of the counsel she received from even her most well-meant advisers. Instead she trusted her own instincts and with a mix of talent, courage, and stubbornness became the celebrated author, poet, lecturer, and educator she is today. Her books for young readers include *Jazmin's Notebook, Growin',* and her latest picture book, *It's Raining Laughter,* illustrated with photographs by Myles C. Pinkney (all from Dial). Born and raised in New York City, she now lives in Seattle, Washington.